BURNT SUGAR

THE NEVER AFTERS

Burnt Sugar

The New Wife

After Midnight

Braid

By The Moon's Good Grace

Winterbloom

BURNT SUGAR

A NEVER AFTERS TALE

KIRSTYN M^cDERMOTT

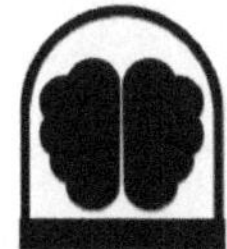

Brain Jar Press
PO Box 6687
Upper Mt Gravatt, QLD, 4122
Australia
www.BrainJarPress.com

Cover design by Peter Ball
Cover Image: *Decorated gingerbread star*, ER_09/Shutterstock;

ISBN: 978-1-922479-19-8 (Ebook) | 978-1-922479-20-4 (Chapbook)

BURNT SUGAR

My brother stumbles through the back gate while I'm still in the hen-house, plucking smooth, warm eggs from dirty straw.

"Them old girls earn their keep this morning?" He tugs at my skirts, flips them up about my wrinkled knees like he always does when he's in his cups, or climbing out of them, like we're still children and always will be. My hands are full; I can't swat him away.

"More than some," I say, passing him a handful of eggs.

He makes a face but takes them, cradles them to his chest. I don't ask where he's been all night, or how many coppers I'll need to fork over to redeem his goodwill at the pub. I hope he took up with Berta this time; she looks kindly upon him, for reasons no doubt best left a mystery to sisters, and would have covered his feet as he slept. My brother is always cold.

I find one last egg to tuck into my apron, then head back to the house. The speckled hen with the gammy leg is pecking around near the steps. Hopeful for scraps, she hops towards us, making gentle bok-bok noises. Behind me, my brother lets loose a cry; I turn too late to catch the eggs as they fall from his hands.

"Hansel!"

He looks down at the bright yellow yolks smearing the ground and the toes of his boots. "That bird looked at me slant," he says. He wipes at one boot with the sole of the other.

The speckled hen makes a rush but I shout and shoo her off. Once they get a taste for eggs, they'll crack open every last one that's laid. I make my brother stomp the whole mess into the mud, churning yolk and white and bits of shell together till there's nothing to be gleaned by even the most persistent of beaks. Four eggs gone to waste, which means fewer cakes today. I'll have to make up the loss with boiled sweets and slabs of fudge.

"Sorry, Gretel," my brother says.

"Don't you fret on it." It's been so long since a *chicken* spooked him, I'd stopped paying attention. Fat and flightless, yes, but birds nevertheless. I lay a hand on his shoulder, squeeze my fingers around his knobbly old bones. "Come inside, you. I expect our Dagmar might have put some bacon aside from breakfast."

"Might there be some cinder toffee put aside as well?" My brother's grin is gap-toothed and yellowed, and grows ever more such with each passing year. I'm certain I'll bury him without a single pearl in his head.

"There might."

Mounting the steps, I look back over my shoulder. The speckled hen is scratching around in the mud. Three of her sisters stalk over to see what she's found, their russet-brown plumage fluffed with interest, but she hops away before their greedy beaks can take a piece of her.

"Birds," my brother snorts.

"Birds," I agree, and push him inside.

She was our mother, the woman who led us into the woods, I'm almost certain of it.

I have only two clear memories from Before.

One is the recollection of her large, strong hands about my waist, lifting me up so that I might see the robin redbreast perched on the woodpile outside our window. Her body is soft and smells of fresh-baked bread. The sun is warm on my face. There are pretty yellow curtains. As she holds me, she hums a tune which I've not heard since and which I could not, in good faith, reproduce today.

In the other, she's feeding me a salty broth. I have a sore tooth, or a sore throat, or a fever, and it hurts to eat. She blows on each spoonful before holding it to my lips. *Open wide*, she says. *Else you'll waste away to shadows*. I couldn't tell you the precise flavour of the soup. Some days I imagine it was chicken; at other times I can summon nothing but the greasy taste of mutton to my tongue.

In neither scene can I picture my mother's face.

I worry that memories wear thin, like cloth. That in my desire to hold on to them, in my attempts to retrieve more and more details with which to patch the holes, I'm not carrying out repair work so much as embroidering new threads over the top. Embellishing, with what seems most meet.

My brother, for instance, is adamant that our curtains were never yellow. That they were nothing more than sackcloth hammered in place with rusty tacks. He's equally adamant that the woman was our stepmother. No *real* mother could abandon her own children like that, he insists. Alone in the woods with nothing but a hunk of stale crust in their trembling hands. Certainly not *twice*.

(I never bring our father into such conversations, though he led us into the trees sure as she did. I never ask why his absolution was so readily granted.)

But she *was* our mother. And, sometimes, she was very kind.

I'll never know why she (and our father) abandoned us. By the time my brother and I found our way home from the witch's house, pockets bulging with stolen gems, our mother was dead and buried. From that moment on, all words were my father's to wield and he found none but ill to speak of her.

These days, with the weight and the wisdom of too many seasons behind me, I'm given to suspect foul play. Her death seemed so convenient, his delight in being loosed from the shackles of marriage so bold. The bruises earned in failing to boil water enough for his bath, or by darning his socks without due neatness of stitch, have long since faded but I feel their shadows still. I never speak of such things to my brother; he won't hear any slight against the man who raised us. (The man who abandoned us. Twice.) And next winter our father himself will have been in the churchyard for three decades, so there is nothing to be gained from that quarter.

But I do think he killed our mother. I'm almost certain of it.

The small iron bell above the door jangles and Dagmar leaves off kneading the pastry for her strudels. I stay in my chair by the window, the mid-morning sun warm on my cheek, peering through half-shuttered lashes as the dark-skinned girl approaches the counter. She'd be tall if it wasn't for the way she carries herself, stoop-shouldered and hunched as though she's even older than I am. She's scrawny too, with wrists that a firm handshake might very well snap, and her hair is doing its best to escape the messy, crow-black braids that confine it.

"Miss?" Dagmar wipes floured palms on her apron.

The girl turns and there's no amount of hunching that can hide the growing swell of her belly, not from those that know how to see. "Day-old bread?" she asks.

"Not that kind of bakery, love. We make cakes here, and confections."

"Day-old cake, then?"

Dagmar looks her up and down, then smiles kindly. "Might be something I can find out back, you give me a minute or two." As the woman bustles through the curtain that leads to our living quarters, I already know she's planning to wrap up the fruit slice which was meant for her supper, though it was only pulled from the oven this morning.

The girl wanders the length of the store, darting glances my way as quick as silverfish in sunlight. My lower back tingles with the faint, familiar press of unseen hands but I keep myself still, keep my breathing deep and even. I'm a harmless old woman dozing in her favourite rocker; pay me no mind.

On the counter top, a tray of toffee apples harden to a glossy, irresistible red.

She grabs two or three in each hand before scurrying to the door, left cannily ajar. A graceful hook of her foot, a bump of her hip, and she's through, the bell sounding alarums even as Dagmar returns with a loaf-shaped bundle in her arms.

"Little mouse!" Dagmar turns to me, bewildered. "I was hardly about to ask for coin."

I push myself to my feet, knees creaking along with the old wooden chair. "Little mouse with a sweet tooth."

"Those apples will come as a shock then, once she gets past the shell."

I rub my lips together, recalling the fruit I ate sliced while dunking its fellows into the vat of bubbling, molten sugar. So crisp the flesh, so tart, yet near too sweet for my tongue. I'd rather pickled onions by the jar full, green tomato relish or liquorice, double-salted. Some days, I could drink my own weight in vinegar, such is my craving for sour.

There's a commotion outside, raised voices and the scuffing of boots, followed by a keen-edged shriek. The door flies open again and my brother marches across the threshold, dragging the weeping, dishevelled girl by her braids.

"Caught her!" His eyes are afire, his mouth snarled in triumph.

Dagmar steps forward. "You turn that poor creature loose."

"She's a thief," my brother says, his words slurring into one another. "See?" He wrenches the girl's arm around to show us the sole remaining toffee apple still clenched in a determined fist. The rest are scattered in a trail behind her, lying out on the wooden stoop and rolling in the filth of the street. Ruined beyond return.

"Let her go, Hansel," I tell him.

He glares at me, then pushes the girl to the floor. She cries out, both hands reaching to break her fall, and the toffee apple hits the boards with a dull, sugar-splitting crack. My brother grins. "Dirty thief," he says, and spits on her.

In three quick paces I'm on him, my palm stinging hot across his cheek.

His eyes grow wide, shock and hurt and fury all vying for best seat.

"Go," I tell him. "Leave now and don't come back till there's not one drop of grog left to wring from your sorry self. Don't bother coming back at all, you ever gonna lay hands on someone who didn't lay hands on you first." Dagmar is right by my side now, solid and strong.

"She's a *thief*," my brother repeats. "She *stole* from us."

"There's some of us know a thing or two about thieving." It's a struggle to keep my voice low, to resist the further urging of those hands at my back. "But we've nothing worse here than a girl with a hungry belly. And we do know worse, don't we, brother?"

He makes no reply to that, only grinds his jaw back and forth, swaying a little on his feet.

"Go on, Hansel," Dagmar says softly. "Take a walk, suck some fresh air into your lungs."

My brother points a bony finger at my chest. "World's full of bints with hungry bellies. You can't be feeding every last fucken one of them." He nods, happy with his last words; I keep my mouth shut tight, happy to let him have them. As he leaves, he slams the door so hard behind him that the glass lids of the sweet jars rattle like old teeth.

Dagmar is already helping the girl to her feet.

"Are you hurt?" I ask her.

She shakes her head, brushes off her skirt. "That man your brother?"

"Don't concern yourself with him; he's been drinking."

"And when he's not been drinking?"

"Then he's still my brother."

The girl regards me warily. One hand rests on her midsection.

"You have a fella?" Dagmar asks. "Someone taking care of you?"

"No." That narrow chin juts forward. Defiant, like the prow of a tall ship coming into harbour. "I take care of myself."

"That's good," I say. "And where do you take care of yourself?"

"I find places."

"The elms have yellowed; the snows aren't far behind."

The girl shrugs. "I'll find warm places."

"Seems you don't hold the whole bushel on stubborn," Dagmar says to me. She smiles and takes the girl gently by the hand. "First, little mouse, you need to get some fruit slice and a strong pot of tea into yourself. Then you can help me finish the strudels."

"Strudels? No, I—"

Dagmar clicks her tongue sharply. "Fruit slice. Tea. Strudels. Then run away and find all the warm places you please. If that's what you please."

The girl looks at me, her face thin with suspicion.

"Do you have a name at least?" I ask.

"Rezia."

"Re-zzz-ia." I like the feel of the word as I speak it, the buzz of that small, trapped hiss behind my teeth. "There's an extra cot and room to spare, for as long as you need use of it. In return, we would have your busy hands helping us in the kitchen and around the store. This isn't charity, young lady, it's trade; fair, square and simple." I mimic her earlier shrug. "The choice is yours."

The girl is still frowning, but I've no further patience to press the point.

"Fruit loaf, tea and strudels," Dagmar says. "You're a skinny little mouse, but no matter. A few months round here will soon see you good and fat and strong."

There's a queer pang in my heart as the two of them disappear behind the curtain. I said near those same words to Dagmar herself when she first slipped into my store all those years ago, shifty-eyed and spindle-shanked, more grime than girl till I got a washcloth to her. Only it wasn't a handful of sour toffee apples the little urchin stole and scoffed right out on my own back steps, too starved to run any further. Not toffee apples or any kind of candy, but a fresh-baked tray of gingerbread.

It's been her favourite ever since.

I consider going after my brother with a bag of peppermint humbugs, but I'm tired and it's easier to let myself be steered back to the chair instead. I close my eyes and listen to the sound of tea-making and know that soon Dagmar will bring me a cup of my favourite blend, spiced and steaming, and that I'll continue to sit here, and rock, as those hands move in gentle, approving circles over my back.

It's always easier.

Despite what our father said when I brought it home from the witch's house, the Book isn't bound in the skin of children. It's deer hide, rubbed dark and smooth by countless years of careful, crafty handling, and the pages within are finest vellum.

It belonged to the witch, though she wasn't the first to own it, nor even the second, and now it is mine.

On the day we came back, our father wrenched it from my tiny hands and, cursing the Devil and all the women who cavort with him, threw it onto the fire. I expected the Book to shriek, to scream bloody murder, but it made not even a whimper. As it burned to ash, the stench of scorching sugar filled our little cottage. My brother closed his eyes and licked his lips. Rubies tumbled from his loosened fists. I vomited all down the front of my apron.

The look of disgust on our father's face was short-lived but I saw it. I see it, still.

That night, after all the stolen gems had been counted and gloated over and locked away safe in his sturdy wooden chest, our father tucked us into our beds. He stroked our hair and kissed our faces as he bade us good night, his bristled whiskers scratching at our cheeks. *All one family again*, he told us. *And you, Gretel, you be the lady of the house now.*

My brother fell asleep almost immediately.

But I slid my hand under the pillow, seeking out the hard, foreign shape I felt beneath my skull. My fingers bumped against unblemished leather, brushed across feathered vellum edges. My skin sparked. And I heard them once more, those familiar bookish whispers curling through my ears with the rustle of late autumn leaves. Unintelligible, yet soothing all the same. Coaxing me as they'd done all those weeks in the witch's house. Promises sly and soft: soon, I would know; soon, I would understand; soon, I would *be*.

I'd wanted to rescue my brother, of course I had. My terror for him, and for myself, for the both of us ending up cooked and plated like stray spring lambs, had been real. But that wasn't why I'd pushed the witch into the oven. It wasn't why I'd slammed the iron door with a clang that will echo to my last living breath, or why I'd bolted it against her pounding and her screams.

Content with itself, the Book warmed its covers against my palm.

In the darkness, the smell of burnt sugar lingered. It coated the back of my throat, no matter how many times I swallowed.

It lingers with me, still. The smell of a witch, roasting.

I wake up choking and roll over to spit a ruby into my palm, thankful at least that I didn't swallow the thing. There's no magic in awaiting a return of *that* nature; several doses of cod liver oil and a close inspection of the chamber pot will do nicely.

I feel a faint, insistent pressing on my back. Though it's dark outside, I sit up and nudge my feet into their slippers. I could find my way in this house with both eyes plucked from my head yet I move with care, having no wish to disturb the sleep of my companions on the other side of the room. With Rezia's belly grown so full, Dagmar has taken to the cot, skidding it right up beside her old bed in case she's needed in the night. I can hear the wispy sound of her breathing as I pass.

Rezia is not asleep. Her eyes glitter like pebbles in the moonlight.

I raise a finger to my lips. I'm seldom able to nod off again when I wake in the small hours and the girl is used to me creeping about at night. Often I plod downstairs and begin preparations for the day's baking. Sometimes I simply rock in my chair and watch the gradual lightening of the sky till the others rouse themselves. Tonight, I light a candle from the stove's embers before making my way to the little closet beneath the stairs where

I keep the Book and my father's wooden chest and other sundry things.

There's no lock on the door, and no need for one; it opens to my touch alone.

The Book sees to that, I believe.

Once inside, I drop the ruby into the chest with the rest of the gems. It took its time coming back, this one; I almost suspected it lost. The Book has its roost on a little table wedged into one end of the closet. It waits for me there, exuding an air not so much of patience as inevitability. I lower myself to the three-legged stool that is one of the last sticks of furniture remaining from the cottage where my brother and I lived as children, and open the front cover. Turn to the place where I record the jewels and their travels. Dip goose feather into ink pot and make a small cross next to the most recent entry. All home, all accounted for.

Hands stroke along my spine.

The Book whispers and gloats.

I leaf through the recipes and culinary notes that fill the bulk of its pages, carefully inscribed by several different hands including, most recently, my own. One is newly blank save for a title, *Half-Sour Pickles*. Frowning, I begin to copy down the recipe for the third time. The Book seems to abhor any dish that isn't sweet, but I'm determined to have my favourites recorded and can rewrite them just as quickly as it wipes the pages clean. Perhaps this time the words will be left unmolested.

My half-sour pickles, in particular, are exquisite. The secret is whole coriander seed and a single drop of blood squeezed from my thumb.

A series of moans fall through the cracks in the staircase above my head. I pause to listen, lifting the quill from the page. My brother was struck poorly this week and refuses to leave his bed, refuses even to allow the town surgeon to visit his sickroom for fear of the leeches that might be pressed into service. Our father was much the same way, near the end. There comes another moan, followed by the dull thud of fist against wall.

I hold my breath. I wait.

Till, at last, it comes: Dagmar's resigned and heavy tread as she feels her way through the dark to my brother's room. She will bring him watered wine, if that's what's needed, and sop the fever from his brow with a cold cloth. She will listen to his complaints about the owls that watch from the eaves and reassure him that they possess no fingers with which to unlatch a window. She will tell him that he's safe and she will hold his hand and stay with him till he sleeps again, or till dawn breaks, whichever comes first.

Dagmar has far more patience with my brother these days than I'm able to scrape together. Too many fractious years have seen my own reserves all but exhausted; what little remains must be prudently rationed, doled out only in times of direst need. Not even this crafty Book can deliver a formula for patience, it seems, nor do I know of any merchant who sells it by the pound. With Dagmar, my brother is in good, gentle hands. She is a kinder woman than I've ever been, and some day I'll find the courage to thank her for it.

Beneath my hand, the Book murmurs and wheedles.

It desires me to turn to its end pages, to study once more the wavering, indecipherable script that will shimmer and swell even as my eyes move over it. I've never been able to read what's written there; even the letters, if such queer scribbles can be called such, are foreign to me. All I've ever gained from such attempts are migraines fit to cripple an ox.

I bow my head and continue with the recipe.

Tonight, no matter how sweetly the Book coaxes, I am stubborn. Tonight, I refuse.

That first time, our father had taken two handfuls of opals, turquoises and pearls to a gem merchant three towns away. I doubt he made the best possible trade, but he did well enough to return with plentiful supplies of food and ale, as well as chickens and a milking cow. My brother received a fine hunting bow that he never learned to use properly and for me there was a smart velvet coat, forest green with the softest fox-fur trim, that lasted two winters before I outgrew it.

A month passed and I was out in the yard feeding the chickens when there came an unpleasant popping sensation in my ears. My mouth was suddenly full and, as I parted my lips in surprise, all those pearls spilled to the ground as though from a broken necklace. It was all I could do to beat the excited birds to them.

(When our father later slaughtered an egg-bound hen, I found a pearl in her gizzard. It astonished me, the thought of such a precious thing rolling around inside her all that time, unsuspected.)

The rest of the gems trickled back over the next year or so, landing on my tongue alone or in pairs at any time of the night or day. I could find neither rhyme nor reason for their return, so I simply squirrelled them away in various secret hidey-holes. I never told my father; even at that young age I could sense the peril that infinite wealth might hold for a man such as he. I never told my brother, either.

Nowadays, there's only one merchant I trust with such trade. A southern man with sun-scorched cheeks and a smile I once found winsome, now feel more as a comfort, he travels through our town each spring. We tumbled together often enough in our younger years and, though it never came to more than that, I can still bring to mind the taste of his sweat-salted skin. He accepts my gems in exchange for all manner of goods, some mundane, some wondrous strange, and as much coin as he might spare. I suspect he knows something of their nature, though the subject has never been broached between us, and his reputation has not suffered from their goblin ways.

(I suspect he knows something of magic in *many* of its sly and slippery forms, but we do not talk of this.)

There was a time, one fate-addled summer, when my bloods briefly stopped and I thought I might have something more precious, more startling, than rubies to present on his next visit, but it wasn't to be. The town had a herbalist and midwife by the name of Eufemia back then – a soothsayer as well, according to some – and she helped me through the pain and the mess of it.

Afterwards, she gave me a small clay urn with its stopper newly sealed with wax.

Might fetch some use, such a woman as ye be.

She touched a finger to her nose, and her eyes drilled right to the core of me. I had no wish, and no small terror, to know what she saw. I put the urn away in a low, dark cupboard and didn't so much as look at it till the following spring.

There was no tumbling with my merchant that year, winsome smile or no. I showed him the urn and told him the story, and we held hands and wept a little together. Then we buried the urn beneath a yew tree and never spoke of it again. That might have been the season for me to suggest he loose his mules and settle his restless bones into my store a while; or for him to pat the seat at his side and ask if I would care to see some more of the world as he travelled it. But he didn't ask, and neither did I, and the moment passed as moments do.

Six jewels glitter in my cupped palm: three rubies, two sapphires, and an emerald, small but clear in colour. Enough to send greying eyebrows skyward on a face well-schooled in discretion.

"An uncommon abundance," my merchant says, holding out his hand. One by one, he lifts each gem to the light, squinting through his appraiser's glass. He has seen the rubies and sapphires before, though naturally will not remark on this fact; the emerald I have never shown him. Long ago, my father traded it for the ramshackle house on the edge of town where we all lived for thirteen years till he died. It didn't pop into my mouth till he was buried.

"I find myself with uncommon needs." I push the plate of spice-cakes towards him. He brought me the recipe himself, picked up on his travels along with the vital ingredients, though over the years I've stretched it out of true.

My merchant smiles. "Sweetening the deal?" He chooses a cake and nibbles from one side. His smile broadens.

I tell him what I require, as well as what I would merely wish to have should he manage to come across such items. Only once has he ever failed me, on a request of such exceeding whimsy and so little consequence, I would be churlish to count it against him.

He nods as I speak, pulling on his beard from time to time. I can all but hear the intricate gear-wheels of his mind moving through their tallies and calculations. There is nothing on my list that cannot be provided, he assures me finally. Though certain things will take some time, if I have it to spare. Sadly, he is not carrying sufficient coin on his person, but can arrange delivery of the balance via a trusted colleague. I'm agreeable to all of this, and more than grateful, and so we touch cups and drink tea to seal our terms.

Out in the front of the store, the bell rings and I hear Dagmar greeting a customer. There is laughter between them and talk of shortbread.

My merchant rests his cup on its saucer. "When I arrived, there were three crows perched upon your roof."

"My brother is dying," I tell him.

"The tide rolls out, so that it may roll in once more."

I've never seen any ocean, and have little patience for pretty words just now, so I sip my tea and say nothing. After a moment, he reaches into his robe and places a small cloth-wrapped object on the table between us, nodding for me to take it. There is a muffled tinkling noise as I unwind the swaddling, and soon I'm holding a miniature sceptre of some strangeness, its brass handle decorated with several tiny bells. At its end is mounted a polished orange shaft about the size and shape of my index finger, bent at the tip as though caught in the act of summoning.

"Red coral," my merchant says. "For when the little one's teeth begin to cut."

Rezia has been closeted upstairs all morning. Her son, barely a week old now, hasn't made so much as a whimper. The beaming man at my table almost certainly winnowed his way through the full harvest of town gossip before coming here, but I'm not about to point out such mundanities. In truth, I'm as fond of the aura of mystery he cultivates as he is himself. I smile and shake the device; the sound of bells is high-pitched but not unpleasant. "Are children's rattles made so fine now?"

"At court, such a gift would be commonplace."

"Here, it is anything *but* commonplace." I wrap the rattle up once more and assure him that Rezia will be delighted. Then, holding the teapot in both hands, I refill our cups. Despite my care, I leave a trail of drops on the tablecloth between his saucer and mine; discarded, discoloured pearls that neither one of us will ever retrieve.

My brother died with skin as yellow as pulled taffy. He died thirsty, begging for water but unable to keep even a single swallow in his stomach. The surgeon, dour and wholly unsurprised, pronounced the patient's organs too full of drink already. My brother, he said, was a sponge grown too sodden to sop anything more. It was past the time even for leeches.

I offered feverfew leaves for my brother to grind between his gums, though judging by the manner in which he writhed upon his bed, this remedy did little to dull the pain.

Still, I sat with him, and Dagmar sat with me, and together we witnessed the last breath rattle from within his ribs.

We stripped him, the two of us, then bathed his body with lavender water. His poor belly was swollen fit to give birth, but no meat clung to his bones, and we could move him well enough to change the linens. We would not allow Rezia to come into the room or help in any way; it might bring a curse on her milk, and she has her son to consider.

Dagmar is down in the yard now, burning his soiled garments before nightfall. I can smell the smoke through the open window.

I sit with my brother, alone.

There are tears pricking at my eyes, but I'm afraid to let them loose. Afraid they will fall not for my brother, but for myself. Not from sorrow, but from anger, and from relief. Shame has been a hook in my heart so long, it's startling to feel its tug afresh.

"Hansel." His name catches on my tongue. I clear my throat. "Hansel, do not fret. Look." From my apron pocket, I pull handfuls of small, white stones. Gathered the night before our father moved us into town, I've kept them safe and hidden all these years. A memento of the cottage in the woods which was our home when we were young.

Before and, for a short time, After.

"The curtains were yellow, Hansel. I'm certain of it."

I lay the stones on his bare torso, making a spiral that unfurls from his navel outward. The last is the smallest, barely a pebble, and I warm it between my palms. Then I part his lips and push it gently into his mouth.

"There, my brother," I whisper. "Now you may find your way home at last."

I sit with him, alone, till the room grows dark and I can hear Dagmar creaking up the stairs to fetch me. Outside, an owl screeches. I do not weep.

The almond crescents almost land on the floor as a sudden, sharp push knocks me forward. I take a steadying breath and slide the baking tray onto the bench. The hands are still at my back, pressing, pressing. "Rezia, come turn these out for me."

The young woman sets aside her broom and hurries over. Dagmar, separating eggs at the other end of the bench, throws me a glance. Her brow is furrowed. "Are you not well, Gretel?"

"Well enough," I mutter, already pushing past the curtain. For all her concern, Dagmar knows better than to follow.

I march straight to the staircase closet; there's little profit in pretending I could go anywhere else. The Book is on its table, looking the same as it ever did, and yet somehow utterly different. There is a *liveliness* about it now, like it might begin to throb or glow beneath my touch. My stomach lurches. Sweat beads along my hairline. I sink down upon my stool and turn to the very back of the Book. And, with that, everything changes.

Though the language remains unfamiliar, its squiggled letters like none that I've ever before seen, I find myself now able to read it. My fingers glide over each new line; the pages are warm as flesh through which the blood still flows. The Book whispers, whispers, and I open my mouth to its words. My throat fills with them. My heart, my lungs, my womb.

Touch me in this moment and I will begin to throb. I will glow.

Everything has changed.

Dagmar grabs me in a fierce hug. Her breath tickles my ear. "Must you go?" As though we haven't had this conversation several times over the past month, the past week, the past hour.

"I must," I say again, disentangling myself from her arms.

"I can't think how we're going to fare without you."

"You have all my recipes by heart, Dagmar, and several of your own. The store will fare just fine."

"I'm not meaning the store, you stubborn old goose."

Smiling, I turn and busy myself with checking the cart one last time. It holds everything I'll need – my merchant, as always, having remained true to his word – and will serve as both transport and bed till I reach my destination, wherever that may turn out to be. The mule I bought cheaply from a local horse trader; she is old and white, a colour many consider to be ill luck in her breed. Her name is Pearl, which seems a portent of sorts.

Wrapped in oilskin and tucked safe beneath the driver's seat, the Book murmurs to me. Hands press at my back, then pinch. The sun will soon raise itself over the roofs of the town; time skips ahead of us. I pull a small sack from my apron pocket and hand it to Dagmar. "This will keep you in good stead."

As she peers inside, her eyes widen. "Oh. Oh, my."

"People like sweets, but they don't buy enough to keep two women and a young child from the poor house. Trade those jewels as you need, but only with the merchant who travels up from the south. You will come to no harm with him, I promise."

"No, Gretel, they're yours. You should take them."

I push her outstretched hands away. "I have all that I need."

We embrace again and I look up over her shoulder at the bedroom window, propped open to catch the summer breeze. Rezia stands within its frame, the babe propped on her hip. She's angry with me for leaving and refused to come down this morning to say farewell, but now she lifts her hand, fingers stretching in a small, sad wave.

My throat cinches tight. I raise my own hand in return.

"Come back when it pleases you," Dagmar says, helping me up onto the cart. "You'll always be wanted here, Gretel. Never think it otherwise."

I nod, my throat too dry for words, and slap the reins lightly across Pearl's back. The mule lurches into motion and I steer her down the road that leads west, away from town, out into the woods. Her white rump gleams in the sunlight.

I don't look back, not even once.

We travel too many days for me to keep track.

Three times, the cart wheel becomes bogged and I have to lay twigs and pine needles for the wheels to bite onto. Three times, the woods become impregnable, impassable, and we need to go back some ways before making further progress. Three times, Pearl stops altogether and waits with trembling flanks and ears a'twitch till some unseen danger passes us by.

I've no clear direction in mind, save where the hands guide me.

We fetch up at last in a clearing deep in the heart of the forest. A brook runs nearby, its waters swift and clean, from which Pearl happily drinks her fill. I snack on salted pork and black olives, sucking the brine from my fingers when I'm done.

My new oven is heavy and black. Nothing a good mule can't lower from the cart with the aid of winch and pulley. Only when the oven is safely sited do I unwrap the Book and breathe in the sweet scent of its binding. The first page I'll need is right at the back and I read through it with care, as I have each and every evening for the past week. These sorts of words are slippery; they have a cunning all their own. I would not like to underestimate them.

At last I feel ready.

I fill the oven's belly with slow-burning coals and stoke it to life.

Then I begin to bake, and to build.

Time slinks past unnoticed in my little house by the brook. I bake and carry out repairs as needed. (Some deer possess a surprisingly sweet tooth; there's a squirrel nearby with an eye for candied cherries.) My cupboards always seem to contain the required ingredients, though I never go to market, nor even know where a market might be found.

I sleep, perhaps more than I should, but never dream.

Occasionally, a gem will pop into my mouth and I think of Dagmar and Rezia and the little babe, who surely can't be a babe any longer. I don't remember the colour of his eyes, or his hair. I can barely recall the shape of his mother's smile. So I put the gem away into the chest with the others, and think of other things.

I read the Book. I feel myself expanding.

One winter morning, I trudge out to the stable to find Pearl dead, her white legs long and stiff. It's cold and the ground is frozen so I retreat back into my house. The oven is warm. The cupboards are full. I don't step outside again till spring and, when I do, Pearl is gone. Not even her bones are left. I don't know if wolves came scavenging during the snows, or if this is all the Book's doing, but I'm saddened nonetheless.

I would have liked to bury my mule. I would have liked a grave by which to sit.

Instead, I choose the largest, smoothest pearl from my father's wooden chest and plant it outside the stable. After three days a small shrub grows there. Its leaves are a bright, flagrant green and sugar cubes dangle from its branches.

The Book is displeased at my misuse of its magic. For one full cycle of the moon, my joints swell and my limbs ache and I find it a struggle to move very far from my bed. Anything I eat is soon brought back up again, along with some things that I did not eat at all.

By the time I'm well, the little shrub has withered and died.

. . .

I disregard the noises outside, assuming them to be the predations of yet another deer, till there comes such a violent shove to the small of my back that I stumble and almost fall. My mouth opens and words, which have never been mine to speak, march smartly out of it.

"Nibble, nibble little mouse; who is nibbling at my house?"

The noises cease and a tiny, tremulous voice calls, "The wind, the wind; 'tis only the wind."

For several petrified moments, I can't move, can't think. Then those hands are steering me to the door and I seem to watch, near outside myself, as my own traitorous fingers reach for the latch, and lift it, and pull.

Two children stare at me, jaws agape. The boy, a shrewd-faced lad of perhaps eight or nine, drops the hunk of gingerbread on which he was chewing and takes a protective step towards his sister. The girl is a year or two younger, with eyes round as harvest moons and tangled yellow hair that hasn't seen a comb for days.

"We was hungry," the boy whines.

There's a pinch at the base of my spine. "Poor children." I hold out my hands to the both of them. "Come inside and I'll feed you all that your hearts desire."

Although somewhat out of practice, I do my best. Buttermilk pancakes sprinkled with sugar and piled high with cream and strawberries. Stewed apples and roasted walnuts drizzled with caramel sauce. Vanilla sponge fingers dipped into warm custard. The girl has a lovely smile, a little shy, but mostly grateful. Despite my trepidations, I feel myself warming to her. Around a mouthful of sugar, she asks why I'm not dining with them.

"I don't like sweets. I never eat them."

"Never?"

"Not since I was your age."

The boy doesn't say a word, just sets himself to chewing and swallowing as though the dinner table is a battlefield, laid out for him to conquer. His eyes are as greedy as his stomach; I see them dart about the place, taking stock of my humble belongings. I see them linger on the wooden chest in the corner. Its lid is closed but unlocked.

After the children are finished eating, I wipe their sticky faces and tuck them into my own bed where they snuggle together like a pair of pigeons. I settle into my rocking chair with a crocheted rug draped over my knees. Too perturbed to sleep, I doze but fitfully, and so overhear the boy when he begins to whisper.

He warns his sister not to be so nice to me. I'm nothing but an ugly old witch, who will eat them for her supper. She starts to cry but he shushes her, tells her not to be such a baby, that good little girls are brave and strong and do what their brothers say. In the morning they will sneak off, taking the old wooden chest with them. He's heard about witches from stories; the chest will be full of treasure and their papa will be pleased. The girl wants to know what will happen if the witch catches them stealing from her.

We'll hit her right in her ugly face, he says. *And then we'll burn her. That's what you do with witches who eat children.*

My blood curdles with rage. I wait till I'm sure they're both sound asleep before sneaking over to the bed. The little glutton has gorged himself on so much of my food, he barely makes a murmur as I lift him in my arms and carry him from the house. The stable is dry and not too cold this time of year, and I make sure to bar the door against his escape. At dawn, I take the boy a plate of eggs with buttered toast and find him hunched on a pile of straw in the corner, head in hands. His eyes, when he looks up at me, are red-rimmed and frightened.

"What you gonna do with me?" he asks.

"You?" I point my finger through the bars. "Why, I'm going to fatten you up and have you for my supper." Then I run back to the house before he can see me laughing.

As soon as she awakes, the girl asks after her brother. I tell her that he was naughty and needed to be taught a lesson, but that she is a good girl and can stay with me in the house to help cook and clean, and to learn many fine and wondrous things. And that she can have more pancakes for breakfast if she likes, or else bacon and eggs and fresh-fried tomatoes, red and soft as her heart.

"Whatever you want, child. Tell me and I'll make it for you quick as wishing."

She crosses her arms over her chest. "I ain't hungry."

The girl tells me her name is Gretel. (Of course.)

Her brother is Hansel. (Of course, of course.)

She's very bright, if willful at times, and picks up her letters with remarkable speed. The only pages we have for writing are in the Book, which cleans itself of our lessons each day as if it were nothing more than a schoolhouse slate. Such tricks have ceased to startle, and the girl has taken to reading recipes out loud to me while we cook together. She still makes mistakes, of course, and shows occasional flashes of temper when corrected.

Her brother is dim, but thinks me even dimmer. He continues to believe that he's destined for the stew-pot and thrusts a gnawed chicken bone through the stable bars at me whenever I demand to inspect his finger for fat. If I even think of letting him loose, there is such a pinching at the base of my spine, I can't breathe for the pain.

(This does not excuse the teasing; I don't know why I do that.)

The hands keep a constant pressure on my back, guiding and guarding my movements, though the Book no longer whispers to me. It no longer throbs, or glows. I worry about those pages at the end. I worry that, should I look at them again, I will see only mad, unintelligible scribbling.

My worry is a cage; it closes ever tighter about me.

I've caught the girl staring at the Book, face slack-jawed and blank. When I shake her thin shoulders, her eyes snap back into focus and her gaze sharpens. Her smile has lost its shyness, and its gratitude. I treat her as kindly as I can.

At night, I lie in bed and listen. My house is too quiet. The girl sleeps curled into a ball at my side, the bony ridges of her spine turned against me.

I have never been so afraid.

. . .

There's a crow in the tree outside my kitchen window, its feathers gleaming blue in the morning light. It catches my eye and clacks its flat, black beak. Pretending not to notice the bird, I return my attention to the bread dough on my table and begin to punch down. There's great satisfaction in how it yields and spreads beneath my fists. When my wrists start to ache, I shape the dough into a loaf and set it aside to proof.

At the other end of the table, the girl sits with a hand on the cover of the Book, her fingers idly stroking the leather.

"Shall I warm you some milk with honey?" I ask.

She shakes her head.

"Then we should start your lessons."

Her gaze, when it fixes upon me, is dull and vacant.

Hands press now at my back, nudging me towards the oven. "But first we will bake." I'm at a loss to explain these words, that trip so casually from my tongue. "Will you creep into the oven, Gretel, and make sure it's hot enough for the bread?"

The girl pushes back her chair, rises to her feet. "I don't know how I'm to do it."

"You silly goose!" I want to slap both hands over my mouth, but such an effort is beyond me. All I can do – all I am *allowed* to do – is stand before the oven and draw the bolt. The iron door swings open. A gust of heat washes over me; the fire is well stoked.

"It looks too small." The girl moves around the table. "I don't think I could fit in there."

"It's big enough," I hear myself say. Strong hands turn me around, pushing at my hips, my shoulders, my neck. "Look, I could get myself in." They bend me over, thrust my head forward. Sweat runs down my face; my eyebrows start to singe. There is a rightness to this moment, I feel it. To the vast, inexorable clockwork turning and grinding and falling at last, again, into place. There is a rightness to *me*, to all I have done, and will do once more. I cling to such certainty; it's all that remains.

And yet, as those bare feet sneak up behind me, there comes a stubborn twist of hope.

That *this* time the girl will make a different choice.

That *this* time—

"Stop." The word is scarcely more than a croak, but it's mine. "Stop," I repeat, louder this time, reaching out to grasp both sides of the oven. Hot iron sears my flesh as I struggle against the force that holds me. "Stop." My throat bleeds hoarse from my screams. Sweat slicks my face. Teeth clenched, I drag myself upright and slam the oven door shut. Bolt it, to be safe. Only then, hands curled raw against my breast, do I turn to find the girl not two paces from me. Her eyes are wide and wet with shock. She is so small.

(I was so small.)

"Stop," I whisper. "Enough."

Ignoring the pain that seethes along my arms, I drag the girl back over to the table, back over to the Book. Her face contorts with dread, with fascination. It's like looking into a mirror. "Don't touch," I warn, slapping her little hand away. "Its claws are sunk too deep in you already." Before my nerve can fail, I open the Book to a blank page. Tear it out quick as pulling a child's tooth.

The Book shrieks even louder than the girl does.

I slam the covers closed then push the damnable thing to the floor. "Enough from you," I tell it. "More than enough, to speak it plain." That sets the Book to muttering, a brittle string of sounds like the crunch of dead twigs beneath a boot. Perhaps I've broken something, or fixed it. Perhaps that is one and the same.

Though my poor fingers won't stop trembling, the page folds easily into the shape of a bird with wings outstretched and a thin, upright tail. There's more than a little of my blood smeared within its creases already, but I dab two more red dots in place of eyes. "Fly," I say, blowing lightly across its back. The bird flutters to life, trilling sweetly, and swoops twice about the house before coming to land on the girl's shoulder.

"Oh," she says, astonished. "Dear little thing!"

"It will show you the way home, if you ask it." Drained, I wave towards the wooden chest in the corner. "Fill your apron pockets, then free your brother and leave. Once you are safe, unfold the little bird and put it away; it's fragile and not a toy for children." I glare at the Book by my feet. "Few things are."

The girl follows my gaze; her young face hardens in longing. I remember.

"Listen." I grasp her by the chin, despite the pain and swell of nausea this action brings with it. "When you are grown, when you are a woman and know your own mind, if not your own heart, then you may find your way back to us, if you still wish it. You only need fold the little bird up again and whisper in its ear. It will lead you to me, and to the Book, which I promise to keep safe till that day."

She looks at me doubtfully. But her eyes at least are bright.

"Trust me, Gretel." I let her go then, and wipe away the smudge of my blood from her face. "Please, this once, let me make this choice for us both."

The girl took all the jewels that she could carry, more than enough to keep her family in comfort for years to come. I wonder about her father, whether he is a more honourable man than mine, whether the girl will still have a mother when she and her brother come scampering home with their stories of witches ensconced in gingerbread houses.

And I wonder if there is any sense to make from such questions at all.

The Book is still sulking; it does nothing but grumble.

After three days of sleep and salves, my hands are healed enough to bind in strips of vinegar-boiled cloth as I set about the slow, painful work of packing up what meagre possessions I wish to take with me. I try not to think about my fingers and how the tightening scars have hooked them into talons. How two on my left hand and three on my right have all but melted together in the healing like over-spread biscuits on an oven tray. The finer skills of baking, I fear, will now be lost to me.

I leave the Book till last. It warms beneath my touch as I wrap it in its oilcloth; my hands spark and tingle. "Behave yourself," I admonish. But when I peel back the cloth to see, my injured skin seems pinker and shinier, and the pain has lessened measurably. "Cruel thing, to wait so long!"

The Book hisses at me.

It makes a fair point. I did leave it lying on the floor all this time, abandoned with wounds of its own to nurse. We have both shown a measure of cruelty; who am I to judge which way the scale leans? Still, I do not trust the thing and am careful to wrap it well before placing it into my pack.

I'll shuffle my way back to town, eventually, I don't doubt that. My hands may be crooked and near to useless, but I know how to follow the stars and to watch for moss on the north side of trees. More than anything, I wish to see Dagmar again, and Rezia too. I wish to see how tall and strong the babe has grown. I wish to sit in my rocking chair by the window and listen for the creaking of mule carts in the spring.

All these things mean home to me, and I need no trail of breadcrumbs to find them.

As I leave, I break off a chunk of gingerbread from the roof. It smells as fresh as the day it was baked, though without my presence I fear the rest of the house will soon crumble away. Only the oven will remain, standing black and cold and alone in the heart of the forest. Perhaps it will be found some day, by a woodsman or a traveller straying from the path, and perhaps they will take it with them as a gift for their wife, or for their daughter. I hope so. It's a good oven, well-made and resilient, and it deserves a second life.

ABOUT THE AUTHOR

Photo by Paul Ewins

Kirstyn McDermott has been working in the darker alleyways of speculative fiction for much of her career. She is the author of two award-winning novels, *Madigan Mine* and *Perfections*, and a collection of short fiction, *Caution: Contains Small Parts*. Her stories and poetry have been published in various magazines, journals and anthologies both within Australia and internationally, with her most recent work being *Never Afters*, a series of novellas that retell classic fairy tales. She holds a PhD in creative writing with a research focus on re-visioned fairy tales and produces and co-hosts a literary discussion podcast, The Writer and the Critic. Kirstyn lives in Ballarat, Australia, with fellow writer Jason Nahrumg and two distinctly non-literary felines. She can be found online at www.kirstynmcdermott.com.

ALSO BY KIRSTYN MCDERMOTT

Perfections

Madigan Mine

Caution: Contains Small Parts

Triquetra

THANK YOU FOR BUYING THIS BRAIN JAR PRESS CHAPBOOK

To receive special offers, bonus content, and info on
new releases and other great reads, visit us
online at www.BrainJarPress.com